The Widower Of Darkness 3

Widower Of Death

M.Y. Hauger

Introduction

Several years had passed since tragedy struck. Since then, things have changed. Hugh had grown up and became a fine young man with a wife and family of his own. He had two children, twin boys who were named Oliver and Obadiah.

For the most part, they were a happy family, although there was one thing that Hugh wished could've been different. He missed his grandfather and since the others saw him as the enemy and an outsider, they blamed him for everything that had gone wrong. Because of this, they didn't want Hugh or his family anywhere near him, and it broke Hugh's heart. It was because of his grandfather that Hugh had a family that he loved. His grandfather was the one person who helped Hugh to come out of his shell and because of it, he found love. Hugh and his wife, Olivia, both knew that Endymion wasn't the one who was causing all the problems, but they also realized that it did no good to say anything. No one would listen. Neither of them liked the idea of their sons growing up never knowing who their great-grandfather was or the things he had done to help the family. They hoped that someday, something would change but during that moment, things seemed hopeless.

Chapter 1

Kurtis and several of the other men of the community had left the area on an important mission. They were to return in several days.

Meanwhile, Endymion and Liam had also left the area. Even after all the time that had passed, they still didn't want to give up on the hope of finding the people who had gone missing years ago. They were also determined to find the one who was behind the disappearances and the murders. The last thing that Endymion wanted was for anyone else to turn up missing or worse. He had never gotten over the loss of the love of his life, and he was bound and determined to avenge his wife and all those who had lost their lives.

Chapter 2

As time went on, there was one who was becoming lonelier and because of it, his heart was full of wrath and bitterness. He often took his frustration out on his prisoners. Since he was miserable, he wanted them to be miserable as well. He didn't care that one of his prisoners, which was Conner, actually cared about him. Delano still abused him.

One day, the prisoner decided to confront him.

"What happened to you? Why have you become so angry ?" he asked.

Delano didn't answer him. He was about to strike him, but then Conner grabbed his hand before he got hit in the face. The two of them became quiet as they looked at one another. The other two prisoners, Damien and Zane, glanced at one another before they both looked at Conner and Delano.

"Oh no, not this again." Damien said.

Zane said nothing as he glanced at Damien with an unhappy expression on his face.

"Why in the world would Conner want to engage with him after all that he's done? Delano beats and torments us almost every day, yet Conner still wants to associate with him. He's made himself so vulnerable to Delano that he even willingly takes the abuse that he gives."

"They say that love has no boundaries." Zane said.

"I don't care who he is. Conner shouldn't be allowing him to do this. Delano is an evil, sadistic monster who cares about no one."

"I know, but unfortunately, that's not what Conner sees."

"There has to be something more to it. In the past, Conner wanted nothing to do with no one, yet, when Delano comes around, he literally rushes to him, even if Delano comes to beat him."

"I know. Conner almost acts as though he's doing Delano a favor by submitting to him." Zane said.

"Well, he's not. Delano couldn't care less about him or anyone else."

"I know. He's pure evil."

"The thing is, I get the feeling that if Delano would decide to kill Conner, he wouldn't put up a fight, in fact, I feel like

Conner would willingly allow Delano to bite him.”

“I get that feeling as well, and that’s a sickening and terrifying thought. If Conner is so willing to go that far for him, what else would he be willing to do for him?” Zane said.

Damien glanced at him with an unhappy expression on his face.

Meanwhile, Delano and Conner were at the other side of the room. They both remained quiet as they looked into each other’s eyes. Moments later, the two of them vanished from the dungeon.

Chapter 3

Delano teleported Conner and himself to his room.

"Are you alright?" Conner asked.

"What do you think?" Delano asked.

"That was years ago. Why is it bothering you now?" Conner asked.

Delano started to pace the floor and then stopped, and he started to cry.

"I didn't want to do it. I never wanted to kill her. I was upset and I lost control. She tried to escape me. I should've seen it coming. She kept saying that she wasn't ready and that she wanted more time. She refused to submit to me. I didn't like that she tried to escape me, especially after all that I had done for her." Delano said.

"She was beautiful."

"Yes, she was. She was almost as beautiful as my wife." Delano said.

He cupped his hands to his face for a moment before he looked at Conner and spoke.

"She and I could've had a beautiful thing. We could've stayed in that beautiful house, and we could've had a beautiful family together, but instead, she rejected me." Delano said.

"You've kept this inside you all this time? No wonder you've been lashing out so much."

"I miss having a beautiful woman in my life. I miss having a family. I'm not getting any younger. I want a wife and children."

"Why don't you try to find another woman?" Conner asked.

"Suppose I do find one, and she rejects me. Then what?"

"Find a different one. Surely there would be one out there who wouldn't reject you."

"What if Lela was the only one who wouldn't reject me?"

"You could always hypnotize one."

"No! I told you already that I want one to fall in love with me on her own. I want one to love me for who I am and not because I forced it to happen."

"I'm sure there are plenty of women out there. I'd imagine that you could find at least one who would fall in love with you."

"I suppose it wouldn't hurt to try to find another one. I just wish that things would've worked out with that other one." Delano said.

"Things are bound to work out. As for the other woman? That's in the past, so you need to let that go, so you can find one who will love you and want to be with you."

Chapter 4

It was several hours later when Delano returned Conner to the dungeon. He said nothing to his prisoners as he looked at them, and then he vanished. Damien and Zane both looked at Conner, and then they glanced at one another before they looked at Conner again.

"What are those?" Damien asked.

"What?" Conner said.

"Those cuts."

"They're old."

"No, they're not. I know for a fact that those cuts weren't there when you left here. What happened?" Damien said.

Conner didn't respond.

"Did he do this to you?" Damien asked.

"No." Conner said.

"Would you lie for him?"

"I'm not lying."

"Then, what happened?"

"I did it." Conner said.

"Why?" Damien asked.

Conner looked away.

"It was an accident." he said.

Damien and Zane glanced at one another with unhappy expressions on their faces.

"Is that the reason you went with him?" Zane asked.

"No, I already told you that it was an accident." Conner said.

"Then what's the problem?" Damien asked.

"He was upset." Conner said.

"When isn't he upset?" Damien asked.

"Why was he upset?" Zane asked.

"It was because of something that happened in the past." Conner said.

"What?" Damien said.

"It involved a woman." Conner said.

"What woman would want him?" Damien asked.

"That was the problem." Conner said.

Damien and Zane both had expressions of concern on their faces as they glanced at one another.

"What are you saying?" Zane asked.

"Wait! Did Delano kill her?" Damien asked.

Conner didn't respond.

"Who was she? Did he tell you who she was?" Damien asked.

"He didn't give a name, but what I can tell you was that she was a very beautiful woman, a brunette." Conner said.

"A brunette? Is it anyone we know?" Damien asked.

"No, but I wish I could've known her. I would've wanted her for myself. She was so beautiful. She lived in a fancy house." Conner said.

At that moment, Damien's and Zane's hearts sank.

"No." Zane said.

His eyes filled with tears as he looked at Damien.

"He killed Lilly?" Damien said.

"Who's Lilly?" Conner asked.

"She was the queen, Endymion's wife." Damien said.

"His wife?" Conner said.

"Yes." Damien said.

"I didn't know. I never saw her. The only thing I had to go on were mental images." Conner said.

Damien and Zane both sat down, and they broke down in tears.

"Poor father. He must have been devastated whenever it happened." Zane said.

The two of them said nothing more as they wept bitterly after hearing the terrible news about Lilly.

Chapter 5

It wasn't long after Delano had left the dungeon when he decided to once again search for a potential wife to spend his life with. Without hesitation, he teleported to the neighborhood where Lilly once lived. Delano snuck around because he didn't want to be spotted by anyone. He glanced around before he teleported himself into a house. Then he found a place to hide. Shortly afterward, a blonde-haired woman entered the room. Delano acted quickly and teleported to where he was behind her, and then he snatched her. He left the house, and then he glanced around until he spotted a small house where he decided to hide out. He teleported the woman and himself into the house. It wasn't long until he spotted another woman. When she caught a glimpse of him, she tried to leave, but Delano teleported over to her, and then he took hold of her before she had a chance to escape. Then he took both women and teleported to one of the rooms upstairs. He let go of them before he locked the door, preventing them from leaving the room. Both women started to back away as they kept their eyes on him.

"Endymion?" the blonde-haired one said.

"No." Delano said.

"Then who are you?"

"First, tell me who you are." Delano said.

"Why?"

"I wouldn't ask why. I'm the one who gets to ask the questions here.

Now, let's try this again. Who are you?" Delano said.

"Why is it so important for you to know who I am?"

"Because I want to know your name." Delano said.

"What if we don't tell you?" the other woman asked.

"I wouldn't do that if I were you." Delano said.

"Why are you here?"

"First tell me who you are." Delano said.

"My name is Veda." the blonde-haired woman said.

Then Delano looked at the other woman, who took a step back.

"My name is Jasmine." she said.

"Good, now that I know your names, allow me to introduce myself. My name is Delano."

"Delano?" Veda said.

"Yes."

"Why are you here?" Jasmine asked.

"What do you want with us?" Veda asked.

"I'm looking for a wife." Delano said.

"Excuse me?" Veda said.

"I know, this may all seem so sudden, but you see, I'm looking to settle down and start a family." Delano said.

"You're not serious, are you?" Jasmine said.

"Do I look like I'm joking?" Delano asked.

"No." Jasmine said.

"No, this isn't right. You need to leave." Veda said.

"Why?" Delano asked.

"Because first of all, we don't even know you. Secondly, this is wrong." Veda said.

"I see nothing wrong with this. Furthermore, you should feel privileged." Delano said.

"Why?" Jasmine asked.

"Because I've chosen the two of you to spend your lives with me. At first, I wasn't sure which one of you to select, but then, as I thought about it, I came up with a solution. Why should I have to choose when I could just have both of you as my wives." Delano said.

"What?" Jasmine said.

"No." Veda said.

"I didn't give you an option. You will both be my wives, and you'll have the honor of carrying my babies." Delano said.

"No, this can't be happening." Veda said.

"It is happening. It's time for us to settle down and start a family. The sooner, the better, after all, none of us are getting any younger." Delano said.

"You're a bit pushy." Jasmine said.

"No, I'm a man who knows exactly what he wants."

"But we can't do this." Veda said.

"Why not?" Delano asked.

"Because I told you already that it's wrong." Veda said.

"Why?" Delano asked.

"Because we're both married." Jasmine said.

"Is that so?" Delano said.

"Yes." Veda said.

"I don't see any men around. Where are your supposed husbands now?" Delano said.

"Are you implying that we're lying to you?" Jasmine asked.

"Perhaps." Delano said.

"We're not lying. We're both married." Veda said.

"Where are your husbands?" Delano asked.

Before they had a chance to respond, Delano spoke.

"No matter. If you truly have husbands, I'll just eliminate them both whenever they return." Delano said.

"No." Veda said.

"Perhaps I should eliminate all the men in this neighborhood so that every woman here could be my wife." Delano said.

"Are you sure you're not Endymion?" Veda asked.

"I can promise you that I'm not Endymion. I look forward to the day when I run into him again. How I would love to sink my teeth into him. All it would take is one bite, and he'd be a dead man." Delano said.

Veda had an expression of horror on her face as she took a step back.

"Is there a problem?" Delano asked.

"You." Veda said.

"What about me?" Delano asked.

"You're the one who's been killing people. You killed Aston's mother. Didn't you?" Veda said.

"Aston's mother?" Delano said.

"Yes."

"Ah, yes, Aston. I remember him. I tried to murder him, but then some guy showed up and interfered with my plans. I'm assuming that it was his dear old dad." Delano said.

"You tried to kill Aston?" Veda asked.

"Yes, I couldn't let that future warrior come into existence. As for the woman, I didn't know that she was his mother. That would mean that she was Endymion's wife."

"Why did you kill her?" Jasmine asked.

"She didn't give me what I wanted." Delano asked.

Veda and Jasmine glanced at each other nervously.

"I didn't want to kill her. It was her fault. She should've never tried to escape me." Delano said.

"What about my sons? Did you have anything to do with their disappearances?" Veda asked.

Delano didn't respond.

"Where are they?" Veda asked.

Delano didn't answer.

"Where are Cullen and Damien?" Veda asked.

"Damien? Do you mean to tell me you're Damien's mother?" Delano said.

"Yes. Where is he? Is he alive?" Veda said.

"Maybe." Delano said.

"What about Cullen?" Veda asked.

Delano didn't respond.

"Did you kill him?" Veda asked.

Delano remained silent as he looked into her eyes.

"Why won't you answer me?" Veda asked.

Her eyes welled up with tears as she looked at Delano.

"Don't cry. You see, we can help each other out. We can begin a new family. Perhaps, I could even let you visit Damien now and then." Delano said.

He tried to kiss Veda, who turned her face.

"Don't be like that." Delano said.

"Why would you think that I would willingly allow you to kiss me? You're a murderer." Veda said.

"I already told you that I didn't want to kill her." Delano said.

He looked into her eyes as he touched the side of Veda's face before he took hold of it. Then he closed his eyes as he kissed her. Then he looked at Jasmine, who started to back away from Delano until he used his powers to cause her to gravitate toward him. When she approached him, Delano looked into her eyes before he closed his eyes and kissed her.

"What do you say? This could be the start of a beautiful thing with just the three of us." Delano said.

Neither woman said a word to him.

"I'm trusting that neither of you will make the same mistake that the other woman made." Delano said.

Both women looked at him with fearful expressions on their faces. Neither of them knew what to do because they were trapped as Delano's prisoners.

Chapter 6

Veda and Jasmine hated being stuck in the bedroom with Delano, who refused to let either of them out of his sight. They wanted to escape and try to get help, but they weren't sure how they would do it, since they both knew that he was able to teleport. They both glanced at the window before they looked at Delano, who was watching both of them closely. Then the women looked at one another nervously. They both wanted to say something, but they were afraid to since they knew that they were being watched. Tension rose inside of them as they watched Delano, who moved toward them. They looked at one another before they started to back away from him.

"Is there a reason that you feel the need to avoid me?" Delano asked.

He continued to move toward them.

"It won't do either of you any good. As you can see, there is no escape."

"Why do you keep us locked in this room?" Jasmine asked.

"I want to keep a close eye on the two of you." Delano said.

"What if we would need to leave the room?" Veda asked.

"You're not leaving this room without me." Delano said.

"What about if we need something?" Jasmine asked.

"I can provide all your needs." Delano said.

"This is like a prison." Veda said.

"It doesn't have to be, but you must prove to me that you won't try to escape me. You must also gain my trust. It won't come easy after what happened the last time." Delano said.

"You shouldn't have expected her to want to stay with you. She was a married woman, just as we are." Jasmine said.

"So? That's not my problem. It was hers." Delano said.

"What about her husband?"

"I couldn't care less about him or how he feels. I have a feeling that the two of you really don't care, either. As for your husbands, I don't care about them either, and it will give me great pleasure to remove them from the situation." Delano said.

"How could you be so heartless? You take people's lives, and you have no remorse for what you do. Meanwhile, someone else has been taking the fall for your crimes." Veda said.

"Is that so? And who would you be referring to?" Delano asked.

"She's talking about Endymion. Everyone thought that he was the one doing these terrible things, but it turns out, he's innocent. It's too bad nobody would listen to him." Jasmine said.

"Is that right? Perhaps, he may be useful to me after all. I was thinking about killing him, but it seems that he serves a much better purpose than I realized, as my scapegoat."

"That's not fair!" Jasmine said.

"I don't care." Delano said.

"I feel so terrible. All this time, Endymion had been treated like an outsider. He was blamed for kidnapping and murder." Veda said.

"Aww, poor baby." Delano said.

"If only we had known the truth before." Veda said.

"Why? What difference would it make! Do you think that he's the only one who has been treated as an outcast! Think again! I've been treated that way my entire life, but no one seemed to care, but the two of you will throw a pity party for him! What about me! Do you think I chose to look like this!" Delano said.

"But you've killed people." Veda said.

"Do you think I enjoyed killing her! Believe it or not, I didn't! I didn't want to do it! She hurt me! She couldn't accept me as I am! She just saw me as a monster! That's how everybody sees me! Nobody cares that I actually have feelings!" Delano said.

Jasmine glanced at Veda before she spoke.

"You know what? You're right." Jasmine said.

Delano looked at her with an angry expression on his face.

"It must be hard to go on living your life knowing that everyone sees you as a monster." Jasmine said.

"If only you knew how difficult it truly is." Delano said.

"I know, I can't imagine how it must feel for you."

"As if you even care."

"I don't blame you for feeling that way. I can also understand why you would have trust issues. I can only hope that someday, you could find it in your heart to give us a chance to prove ourselves to you." Jasmine said.

Delano kept his eyes on her as she moved toward him. He looked her in the eyes as he gently touched the side of her face.

"Did you truly mean what you said?" he asked.

"Of course. I wouldn't have said it if I didn't mean it." Jasmine said.

"I'm glad to hear that you've come around to my way of thinking. Perhaps I could give the two of you a chance to prove yourselves to me. I would really like to settle down with both of you." Delano said.

He then gave Jasmine a kiss.

"There's something that I need to do, but I'll be back shortly." Delano said.

Then he teleported away.

Chapter 7

After Delano had vanished, Veda rushed to the door, and then she tried to open it, but it wouldn't budge.

"He did something to the door! I can't open it." Veda said.

She kept trying to open the door, but it still wouldn't open.

"Why did you tell him to give us a chance to prove ourselves to him? I want nothing to do with him and I don't want him anywhere near me!" Veda said.

"Don't you see? This could be our chance to put an end to this." Jasmine said.

"How do you figure that?"

"I have an idea."

"What is it?" Veda asked.

"We need to gain his trust."

"Why?"

"Steve keeps a knife in the drawer of the nightstand. If we can get him to believe that he can trust us, he'll be right where we want him, and he wouldn't suspect a thing."

"Are you saying that we'll have to kill him?"

"Yes."

"I think I'm going to be sick. I've never killed anyone before. I'm not sure if I can go through with it."

"This horrible monster wants to kill both of our husbands. Look at the damage he has done in the past. He murdered Endymion's wife needlessly. Also, Endymion has been getting the blame for everything that has gone wrong. I think it's time we do something about it. We need to clear his name and put an end to all the trouble. If that isn't enough to convince you, think about your sons, who have been missing for years. I think it's time to avenge them." Jasmine said.

"You know, you're right. I've had enough of this. It's time to put a stop to it, even though I feel like this could be really dangerous."

"Being stuck here with him is dangerous." Jasmine said.

"Wouldn't we be further ahead to just climb out the window and try to get help?"

"No, that would be too easy. I feel like he's testing us to see if we'll try to escape. Even if we would be able to get out of the room, more than likely he'll still catch us. I feel like he's hiding somewhere, so he can see what we'll do. There's also the chance of him killing anyone else who's close by. I don't want to put anyone else in danger." Jasmine said.

"You're probably right. It does seem like he conveniently left right after he said he would give us a chance."

"Exactly."

"So, what should we do?" Veda asked.

"For now, we do nothing. We wait until he returns, and then we do whatever it takes to gain his trust and make him happy. Whenever he least expects it, we make our move, and we make sure he never hurts anyone ever again."

Chapter 8

It was several minutes later when Delano returned with a bunch of grapes and other things to eat and drink. He set everything down on the nightstand, and then he looked at both women before he approached them. He took them both by the hand and took them over to the bed before he sat down. Then he gave them both some fruit to eat. He kept his eyes on them as he sat there, and then he lay down.

"Come, sit down beside me." he said.

The two women were hesitant at first, but then they reluctantly did as he asked.

"I'm feeling a bit hungry myself. When the two of you are finished, I would like some grapes." Delano said.

"You can have them. I'm sure there's plenty here for everyone." Veda said.

"I want you to feed them to me." Delano said.

"Very well. As you wish." Jasmine said.

"Does it matter which one of us feeds them to you?" Veda asked.

"I want both of you to feed them to me." Delano said.

Veda and Jasmine glanced at one another nervously.

After they had finished eating, Jasmine took a grape and fed it to Delano. Then Veda took one and fed it to him. As Delano opened his mouth, Veda caught a glimpse of his fangs, and she became even more nervous than she already was. With an expression of horror on her face, she glanced at Jasmine.

"Is everything alright?" Delano asked.

"Of course. Why would you ask?" Jasmine asked.

"I can't help but notice that Veda seems to be terrified of me." Delano said.

Then he glanced at Veda.

"Do I frighten you?" Delano asked.

Veda didn't respond as she tried to give him more to eat. Delano took another bite, and then he took hold of

Veda's hand. He looked into her eyes as he kissed her hand.

"You don't need to be afraid of me as long as you give me what I want." Delano said.

Chills ran down Veda's spine as their eyes met, and then she tried to look away when Delano took hold of her face. He looked into her eyes for a moment before he closed his eyes and gave her a kiss. She felt terrible about what was happening. Her stomach turned as she thought about how hurt Kurtis would've been if he would've known about what was happening. Then she was taken back to when Levi tried to pursue her, even though he knew that she was in love with Kurtis. Feelings of guilt overtook her as Delano continued to kiss her. She wanted so badly for the nightmare to be over. Veda hoped that the moment would soon come when she and Jasmine would take down the horrible monster who held them captive so that they could end the trouble and be set free.

Chapter 9

As time went on, Delano grew tired. He wanted to stay awake, so he could keep an eye on Veda and Jasmine. They could both see that he was tired, and they wanted to try to use it to their advantage. The two of them wanted to make him more relaxed as they hoped that he would fall asleep. They reluctantly made their way over to him and sat down beside him, and then they both gave him a kiss.

"Rest with me." Delano said.

They both did as he asked.

He smiled as he sighed, and then he glanced at each of them.

"It brings me great pleasure to see that the two of you are no longer resisting me. I truly believe that we'll have a beautiful future together." Delano said.

"We both realized that you were right about everything. We both feel terrible about misjudging you earlier. That was our mistake, and we now know that you just want what everybody else wants." Veda said.

"That is true. People seem to overlook the fact that I am human, and I have wants and needs just as everybody else." Delano said.

"We promise not to do that. We're going to take good care of you." Jasmine said.

"I'll take care of both of you. I promise to make both of you happy.

You'll see how loving I can be. I will not disappoint either of you." Delano said.

He then smiled.

"I see a bright future for us. We'll have a beautiful family together. We'll have many children. It'll bring us so much joy. I'll be happy once again." Delano said.

"What do you mean that you'll be happy again?" Veda asked.

"I once had a family, but I lost them all on the same day." Delano said.

"What happened to them?" Veda asked.

"Because I was always seen as a monster, people often tried to destroy me. One day, I was out with my family and some men came along. They started shooting at me with their bows. My wife quickly got in front of me, resulting in her getting shot instead of me. She ended up dying in my arms.

Then, to make things worse, the same men went after my sons because they wanted to kill them. They saw them as monsters too, so they wanted to destroy them. I searched for them, but I never found them." Delano said.

"We're so sorry. We had no idea how tragic your life was. It must have been devastating to lose everyone like that." Jasmine said.

"It was devastating. I still miss them."

"If only there was something we could do to help you." Veda said.

"But there is something that you can do. Together we can begin again. We can start over and have a family. The two of you can give me another chance at happiness." Delano said.

Jasmine took hold of Delano's hand, and then she spoke.

"We promise to make you happy.
We won't let you down."

Chapter 10

Several hours had passed, and Delano had fallen asleep. Veda opened her eyes and glanced at him before she looked at Jasmine, who was also awake.

"Is he asleep?" Veda asked.

"I think so." Jasmine said.

Then Veda got up from the bed and made her way over to the nightstand. When she approached it, she glanced at Delano before she opened the drawer and took the knife out.

"I guess it's now or never." Veda said.

She made her way back over to the bed. As she looked at Delano's face, her heart sank as she thought about what he had told them about his family.

"I don't know if I can go through with this." she said.

"We have to. It's the only way out of this. We need to end this now. We said we were going to take good care of him, and that's exactly what we need to do. It's time to give him exactly what he deserves." Jasmine said.

Veda looked at Delano as she was hesitant to go through with the plan. Then she started to think about when he said that he would kill Kurtis and Steve. Then she thought about how Endymion was constantly getting accused of things he never did. She thought about her sons, who she hadn't seen in years. At that moment, Veda became angry, and she took the knife and stabbed Delano in the abdomen. Delano opened his eyes, and then he let out an agonizing holler. Before he had a chance to move, Jasmine acted quickly and held him down. Delano's eyes filled with tears as he looked into Veda's eyes. She could see that he was devastated about what was happening, as he looked at her helplessly.

"Cover his face." Veda said.

Jasmine acted quickly and took a pillow and put it over Delano's face. Veda stabbed him several times. His voice was muffled by the pillow that Jasmine had on his face as he cried out in pain. Eventually, Delano became silent and he was motionless. Veda and Jasmine looked at one another before Jasmine removed the pillow from Delano's face. They noticed that his eyes were closed.

"Is he dead?" Veda asked.

"He's not breathing." Jasmine said.

Veda checked for a pulse.

"He's dead." Veda said.

"Let's get out of here and tell the others." Jasmine said.

She and Veda made their way to the door and tried it, but they couldn't get it open. Then they rushed to one of the windows. As they tried to open it, Veda glanced at the bed and noticed that Delano wasn't there. She suddenly found herself trapped in someone's strong arms, and she became terrified because she knew that it could only be one person who was holding her tightly.

"You shouldn't have done that. You led me on, and then you tried to kill me. How could you do this to me?" Delano said.

Veda trembled as Delano held her close to him. He kissed her cheek before he spoke into her ear.

"It's too bad that you tried to kill me. I can't let that go. You've shown me that I can never trust you, and you leave me with no other choice." Delano said.

Jasmine tried to get Veda freed from Delano's arms, but it was too late. He sank his teeth into Veda as he hugged her tightly. She could feel herself slipping away. Moments later, he released her, and she fell to the floor. Jasmine trembled as she glanced down at Veda, and then she looked at Delano, who had a blank stare on his face as he kept his eyes on her. She took a chair that was in the room and threw it at him, but it didn't stop him. Jasmine rushed over to the other window and tried to open it. Suddenly, Delano was gone. Jasmine's heart pounded in her chest as she looked around. Then suddenly, Delano was right beside her. Before she had a chance to get away, he took hold of her, and then he bit her. Moments later, she fell to the floor. He glanced at her angrily before he vanished from the room, leaving them both behind.

Chapter 11

Delano went back to his home. Tears ran down his face as he thought about how the two women had tried to kill him. He winced, and he groaned as he put his hand on his abdomen. When he looked at his hand, he noticed that it was covered in blood. Without hesitation, Delano teleported to the dungeon.

"Oh no, it's him again." Damien said.

When Conner glanced at Delano, he became concerned as he noticed that he appeared as though he was in pain. Conner got up and rushed over to Delano, who had his hand on his abdomen. When he approached him, he took hold of his hand and he became devastated as he noticed that it was covered in blood.

"You're hurt." Conner said.

As Delano looked at Conner, he started to bleed from his nose and mouth.

"What happened to you?" Conner asked.

"I was attacked. They tried to kill me. One of them stabbed me while the other tried to smother me with a pillow." Delano said.

"Thank goodness you managed to escape." Conner said.

"Yes, but needless to say, they weren't so lucky." Delano said.

"What happened? Did you kill them?" Zane asked.

"They left me with no choice. They would've killed me had I not killed them."

"Does it really have to end with you murdering someone?" Damien asked.

Delano didn't respond as he started to cough.

"You need help." Conner said.

Delano glanced at him before he took him and disappeared. Damien had an expression of disgust on his face as he shook his head.

"You know, I'm growing a little sick and tired of Conner catering to him as he does. Delano just said that he killed people, yet he still puts him on a pedestal." Damien said.

"I know. I realize that Delano claimed that he was attacked, making it sound like it was self-defense, but do you believe it?" Zane said.

"I'm not buying it. Even if he was attacked, I have a feeling that there was more to it, and he's not telling us everything."

"You're probably right."

"I guarantee that I'm right. Whatever went on, I have no doubt that Delano was the one who provoked it."

"It wouldn't surprise me, after all, he seems to take pleasure in everyone else's pain." Zane said.

"Delano is far from innocent. The question is, who did Delano kill and why?"

"Do you think we'll ever find out?" Zane asked.

"I'm not certain, but whatever it was that happened, I have a feeling that Conner will know about it. Hopefully, he'll tell us what happened.

Chapter 12

Meanwhile, Delano and Conner were in Delano's room. Delano winced as Conner helped him onto the bed. Without hesitation, Conner unbuttoned Delano's shirt, so he could clean his wounds. Conner fought back tears as he looked at the number of times that Delano had been stabbed. While Conner started to clean the wounds, Delano turned his face as his eyes welled up with tears. He didn't want Conner to see that he was about to cry.

"What happened out there? Why did they attack you?" Conner asked.

Delano didn't respond as he covered his face with his hands. Tears filled Conner's eyes as he continued to clean Delano's wounds.

"I hate that they did this to you. How could they be so cruel?" Conner said.

"They attacked me for no reason. I had done nothing to them. They led me on, giving me the impression that they wanted to be with me, but it turns out they had plotted against me. They turned on me and tried to kill me." Delano said.

Conner cleaned the blood from Delano's face.

"They were women?" Conner asked.

"Yes. I went back to the neighborhood to find a wife. Unfortunately, I found more trouble instead." Delano said.

Conner sighed as he looked at Delano's wounds before he looked into his eyes.

"I suppose that you'll turn against me now. The thing is, it's not that I enjoy murdering women. They left me with no choice." Delano said.

He then broke down and cried.

"They broke my heart. They played me just so they could try to kill me. They didn't even show any remorse for what they were doing. The one who stabbed me looked me in the eyes before she told the other one to cover my face." Delano said.

"It sounds to me like it was self-defense. You just said that they attacked you. Did you not?" Conner said.

"Yes."

"Had you not defended yourself, they may have killed you instead."

"I'm certain that they would have. As I said, neither of them showed any remorse for what they did. The one who stabbed me kept doing it while the other one held the pillow over my face. The only reason they had stopped was that they thought that I had died." Delano said.

Tears rolled down his face as he closed his eyes, and then he opened his eyes and looked at Conner.

"All I wanted from them was for them to share their lives with me and to have my children. I had done nothing to them to prompt them to try to murder me as they did." Delano said.

"I'm really sorry."

"I'm beginning to wonder if I'm wasting my time. I truly hoped that I could've found someone to spend my life with, and I wanted to start over, but no one will give me a chance."

"Perhaps you just haven't found the right one."

"I'm starting to feel like there is no other one. Lela was the only one who ever gave me a chance. She was the only one who loved me for who I was. Everyone else in this world sees me as a monster."

"I know that you're not a monster, in fact, there probably isn't a single person who knows that as well as I do."

"To be honest, I'm shocked, and a bit confused about why you're not judging me. Anyone else would. I'm sure that the others have." Delano said.

"But I'm not them. I understand that you had to defend yourself. I can't judge you for that." Conner said.

"Why not? Why are you different from the others?"

"You know the answer to that. I see that you're still in denial."

"You don't know all that there is to know, even though you act as though you do."

"I could never judge you. The fact is, I don't want to lose you. For so long, I was led to believe that you were dead and that I would never see you again. Thankfully, that wasn't true."

"I'm not who you think I am." Delano said.

"I know exactly who you are. You can say what you want, but I know that it's you. For some reason, you've forgotten who you are. If only you could somehow remember."

"The only thing that I can remember is nothing but heartache and pain. Everything near and dear to me has been torn away from me. So many years had passed, and all I wanted was a second chance. I wanted to start over again, so I could have a family. The ones I took years ago had grown up. I put them back into the dungeon because I don't want them to leave. They've never implied that they would, but I can't take any chances. I love them as my sons, but I still want to have sons of my own. It seems so hopeless, but I don't want to give up because I'm so tired of being alone."

"But you're not alone." Conner said.

"I want a family. I want a woman to spend my life with and children to take care of. I miss that. You would never understand."

"But I do understand."

"Do you?" Delano asked.

Conner said nothing as he looked at him with a sorrowful expression on his face.

"I'm a lonely man. So much had been taken away from me. I missed the first years of my youngest sons' lives. I felt so cheated. Now, they're not even here. I had hoped for another chance; an opportunity to have a family that I could enjoy without being separated from them."

"Then don't give up."

"What's the use in trying? Lela was the only one who ever loved me for who I am. She was my best friend. There was no one like her, nor will there ever be another like her ever again."

"No, I don't doubt that for a minute, but if you just give up, you'll never know if there's someone else out there who could be interested in you."

"I've already been rejected by three of them. I'm not sure if I can deal with being rejected anymore."

"They weren't the right ones."

"I truly wish the first one would've been the right one. She was so beautiful. They were all beautiful. Why couldn't they feel the same way about me?"

"They didn't happen to mention whether they were married, did they?" Conner asked.

"Yes."

"That could be a huge part of the problem right there. Perhaps you could try finding one that isn't married."

"Their husbands weren't even there." Delano said.

"That makes no difference. Most likely, they were wanting to remain true to their husbands. Would you have wanted a man to come along and try to steal your lover from you?"

"One did try to steal my lover from me. Needless to say, he didn't get away with it."

"What about her?" Conner asked.

"She refused to be with him, even when she thought that I was dead."

"See? It very well could've been the same for the three women who didn't want to be with you. I would never condone them trying to kill you, but you can't exactly blame them for not wanting to be with you."

"No man is going to stand in my way if I see a woman that I'm interested in."

"But you'll never win a woman over if you kill her husband. Most likely, she would despise you because of what you had done. That's why you need to find one that's not married or in any kind of relationship with a man."

"What would you suggest, since you think you're so smart?" Delano asked.

"Maybe you could try looking elsewhere. More than likely, the neighborhood where you keep going isn't a good place for you to find a wife. There aren't that many women there, and most of the ones who are there are taken."

"There has to be one that's available."

"I truly believe that you should go somewhere else, otherwise, you'll just keep shooting yourself in the foot."

"Perhaps you're right." Delano said.

"I am right. Just think about what I'm telling you. Go somewhere else where you can find one that isn't married. You would probably have a better chance of finding one that may become interested in you. Just don't give up."

Chapter 13

The following day, Delano took Conner back to the dungeon.

"I think you should take some time to rest." Conner said.

"You're probably right." Delano said.

"Why don't you sit down with me?" Conner asked.

"Must I?" Delano asked.

"I agree. Must he?" Damien said.

Delano looked at Damien angrily before he spoke.

"On second thought, I may stay here for a bit. I see that Damien really enjoys my company. I wouldn't want to disappoint him." Delano said.

Damien glared at him as he sat down.

"I don't plan to stay for very long. I want to continue my search for a wife." Delano said.

"Are you kidding me? You don't deserve a wife after what you did to Lilly." Damien said.

"I wasn't speaking to you, so stay out of it."

"Why did you kill her?" Damien asked.

"She rejected me."

"She was married! What did you expect her to do?"

"I expected her to submit to me, but instead, she tried to escape."

"What about the two people that you killed yesterday? Were they also women who rejected you?" Damien asked.

Delano said nothing as he looked Damien in the eyes.

"Who were they?" Damien asked.

Delano didn't respond.

"Tell me!" Damien said.

"Very well. If you must know, suit yourself. One of them was named Jasmine." Delano said.

Damien got choked up after he found out that one of Delano's victims was Steve's wife. He fought back tears as he looked Delano in the eyes.

"Who was the other one?" Damien asked.

Delano stood up, and then Damien stood up.

"Where are you going? I asked you a question." Damien said.

"I think it's time that I left. I have things to do." Delano said.

Zane glanced at Conner before he stood up.

"Not so fast. I want to know who she was, and I want to know now!" Damien said.

"Very well, her name was Veda. I'm certain that you know who that is, don't you, Damien." Delano said.

At that moment, Damien's heart sank.

"You killed my mother?" Damien said.

Zane's eyes welled up with tears as he glanced at Damien, who looked at Delano angrily.

"She tried to kill me! She was the one who stabbed me, and she wouldn't stop!"

"No! You monster!" Damien said.

With tears running down his face, he ran toward Delano as he was about to fight him. Delano used his powers to knock him down to the floor. Damien cupped his hands to his face as he wept.

"Aww, is the poor baby crying for his mommy?" Delano said.

With an expression of fury on his face, Damien got up and rushed over to Delano, and punched him. Then he struck him again, knocking him to the floor. Damien started beating him, but then Delano vanished, and then he reappeared before he punched Damien before he used his powers to knock him down.

"Enough!" Delano said.

Damien looked up at him with an expression of fury on his face. Tears were streaming down his face.

"She attacked me! She tried to kill me! That wasn't my fault!" Delano said.

"You should've known that she wouldn't want to be with you!" Damien said.

"She toyed with me! They both did! They led me on, leading me to believe that they wanted to be with me! It was just a plot for them to gang up on me, so they could murder me!" Delano said.

He then took hold of Damien, pulled him up, and punched him, knocking him back down to the floor.

"That's for your mother for trying to kill me!" Delano said.

He then took hold of Damien again before he punched him a second time.

"That one's for your father!" Delano said.

Then he kicked Damien in the abdomen.

"That one's just for you. Next time, you better think twice about trying to fight me. I won't be so easy on you next time." Delano said.

Damien said nothing as he looked at Delano with tears running down his face.

"You've been a lot more trouble than you're worth, Damien. I'd kill you, but I like seeing you cry. Your pain brings me pleasure." Delano said.

Damien cupped his hands to his face as he wept bitterly. Delano said nothing more as he stood there and looked at him for a moment. Then he glanced at Conner before he vanished from the dungeon. Zane made his way over to Damien, knelt down beside him, and hugged him as tears ran down his face.

"I am sorry." Zane said.

"I can't believe that my mother is gone because of that horrible monster. And what about my father? He must not have been home when it happened." Damien said.

He then looked at Zane with tear-filled eyes.

"He's going to be devastated when he goes home and finds that she's been murdered. To make things worse, your father is probably going to be the one who gets the blame for it." Damien said.

Zane had a sorrowful expression on his face as he looked down at the floor.

"We both know that your father isn't the one who's causing the trouble." Damien said.

"But that isn't enough. Delano must be stopped. Unfortunately, I'm not sure if we could ever defeat him. Our fathers may be our only hope. If only they could set aside their differences so that they could join forces and defeat Delano before he hurts or kills anyone else."

Chapter 14

After leaving the dungeon, Delano decided to head back to the neighborhood where he murdered his last two victims. He teleported himself to the area, and then he glanced around before he snuck around. Delano was careful because he didn't want to be seen. He made his way to a house where he had not been before. As he glanced in one of the windows, a woman caught his attention. He glanced around before he teleported into the house. Delano listened for a moment before he went upstairs. He went into one of the bedrooms and hid in one of the closets. Suddenly, the woman came into the room. Delano remained in his hiding spot for a moment, and then he crept out of the closet. He quietly made his way to the door and locked it. When he turned, he noticed that the woman was standing there looking right at him.

"Endymion? Is that you?" she asked.

"No." Delano said.

"Then who are you? What are you doing here?"

"I feel like I've seen you somewhere before. Your face looks familiar."

"I asked you a question. Who are you?"

"Isn't your name Olivia?" Delano asked.

"How do you know my name?"

"So, I have seen you before."

"Why can't you tell me who you are?"

"It's all coming back to me. It was several years ago. We were in another part of the world."

"I don't know what you're talking about. I don't even know who you are." Olivia said.

"But I do know you. You caught my attention years ago, but you were with somebody else at the time. How did that work out for you? And how in the world did you end up here?"

"That was in the past."

"What are you doing here? I know for a fact that you broke it off with your precious beau."

"It didn't work out. We both moved on."

"Can I let you in on a little secret?"

"What secret?" Olivia asked.

Delano smirked before he moved closer to her. He put his arms around her before he spoke into her ear.

"I caused the two of you to split up." Delano said.

Olivia broke free, and then she backed away from him.

"It's true. I caused you to turn against him. I put it in your head that he would arrest you if you ever broke up with him. I also caused you to believe that he's an evil tyrant who arrests people for every silly thing. It was also I who was chasing you, not him." Delano said.

"Why, how could you?" Olivia said.

"Does it even matter anymore? That happened years ago."

"Why would you do such a thing?"

"For the same reason that I'm here now. I'm a lonely man. I long for the companionship of a woman. It's been so many years since I've had the attention that I yearn for." Delano said.

"You've come to the wrong place, and I think you should go."

"I've had everything taken from me. Do you know what that feels like?"

"No."

"I want to start over. I want a wife to spend my life with. I want children that I can enjoy and love." Delano said.

He started to move toward Olivia, who backed away from him as she kept her eyes on him.

"I've noticed that you're alone." Delano said.

"No."

She continued to back away from Delano, who kept moving toward her. He kept moving closer to her until he had her cornered. Olivia wanted to get away from him, but there was no escape. Then Delano took hold of her as he looked into her eyes.

"I want you to be my wife and the mother of my children." Delano said.

"No. Please, don't." Olivia said.

"That's the whole reason I sabotaged the relationship between you and that other guy. No man stands in my way."

"But you can't do this."

"Why not?" Delano asked.

"I'm married."

"That's never stopped me before." Delano said.

He tried to kiss Olivia, who turned her face.

"I wouldn't do that if I were you." Delano said.

"Please, don't do this. I told you already that I'm married. I love my husband and I want to remain true to him."

"I'm warning you. If I were you, I wouldn't reject what's in front of you."

"Why can't you just go away?"

"I will not leave without getting what I want."

"I will not be your wife, nor will I have your children. I told you already that I'm married."

"Where is your husband now?" Delano asked.

"He went away for a few days."

"Is that so?"

"Please, just go."

"No." Delano said.

Olivia tried to get away from him, but she couldn't get free from him. He took her in his arms and held her tightly.

"Let go of me!" Olivia said.

She squirmed as she tried to escape Delano, who started to move toward the bed, even as he kept hold of her. When he approached the bed, he put Olivia onto it. Then he got onto the bed and as he moved close to her, Olivia kicked Delano, causing him to holler. Olivia quickly got off the bed, ran to the door, and tried to open it, but it wouldn't open. Delano got up, and with an angry expression on his face, he made his way over to Olivia, who then ran to one of the windows. She unlocked the window, but then Delano approached her and took hold of her.

"I told you not to do that! I warned you about rejecting me! Also, you kicked me! That wasn't very nice!" Delano said.

"Please, let me go." Olivia said.

"No! We could've had a bright future together, but instead, you hurt me. I can't let that go." Delano said.

He kept hold of her as he sank his teeth into her, even as she tried to get away from him. Her struggle became less and less as Delano kept hold of her. Within moments, Olivia became motionless, and then Delano took her over to the bed and put her down. He looked at her with an unhappy expression on his face.

"It's a shame. We could've had a beautiful life together. Because you rejected me, your life is over." Delano said.

He was about to leave when, suddenly, he heard a knock on the door followed by the voice of a child.

"Mother?" the child said.

"A child?" Delano said.

The boy knocked on the door again.

"Mother? Are you alright?" the child said.

Delano suddenly became curious about the child who was trying to get into the room, so he unlocked the door before he hid in one of the corners of the room. The child, not suspecting anything, opened the door and entered the room.

"Mother? Are you alright?" the boy said.

He spotted Olivia on the bed and rushed over to her. When he approached her, he gently shook her.

"Mother?" he said.

Then he noticed a bite on her and his heart sank. He checked for a pulse, but found none.

"Mother." the child said.

At that moment, the child broke down in tears as he hugged Olivia. He didn't notice that Delano crept over to the door, closed it, and locked it. With tears in his eyes, the child got up from the bed and was about to leave the room to get help when he spotted Delano in the room looking right at him.

"Where are you going?" Delano asked.

The child became tense as he looked at him.

"What's your name?" Delano asked.

The child didn't answer.

"I asked you a question, boy. Who are you? I want to know your name." Delano said.

Tears ran down the child's face as he took a step back.

"Don't make me ask again." Delano said.

"Please, let me go." the child said.

"Answer me!"

"M...my name is Oliver."

"Oliver? Was Olivia your mother?" Delano asked.

Oliver started to cry as he glanced at his mother and then took a step back.

"Who's your father?" Delano asked.

Tears ran down Oliver's face as he kept his eyes on Delano.

"Your father wouldn't happen to be Endymion, would it?" Delano asked.

Oliver shook his head.

"Who's your father?" Delano asked.

Oliver didn't answer.

"Is it Aston?" Delano asked.

Oliver shook his head.

"No. He's my grandfather." he said.

"Your grandfather?"

"Yes."

"What's your father's name?" Delano asked.

Oliver began to tremble.

"Answer me!" Delano said.

"His name is Hugh." Oliver said.

Delano scoffed.

"What? You must be joking. Did I just hear you say that your father's name is Hugh?" Delano said.

Oliver didn't respond as he broke down in tears.

"I don't believe this. Did she marry the crybaby? You're his son? I thought he died years ago." Delano said.

Tears rolled down Oliver's face as he glanced at his mother and then looked at Delano, who suddenly seemed angry.

"No. This will never do. I should've known that it was all too good to be true. Nothing is ever that easy, now, is it? I should've known it from the start, I mean, it was obvious that your father was connected to Endymion somehow, but I would've never guessed that he's Aston's son. Well, this changes everything. Something is going to have to be done about you." Delano said.

"No, please, let me go." Oliver said.

"No, I'm afraid I cannot do that. For all I know, you could be that future warrior that everyone was talking about. Even if you're not him, I remember hearing about him being born through your family. If it's not you, he could come through you. I cannot allow that to happen. I must see to it that he never exists." Delano said.

He then glanced at Olivia before he looked at Oliver.

"This is perfect. They'll think that you did it to yourself." Delano said.

"No, no. Please don't." Oliver said.

Delano started to move toward Oliver, who made his way over to the window. He opened it and was about to climb out, but then Delano approached Oliver and shoved him, causing him to fall out the window. Oliver hollered as he fell to the ground. Delano teleported to where the child had fallen. When he saw that Oliver was unconscious, he vanished, leaving the child behind.

Chapter 15

Delano went back to his home. He thought for a moment before he teleported to the dungeon. Damien didn't notice that Delano had returned since his hands were covering his face as he wept. Zane was trying to comfort Damien, and Conner just sat there quietly. When he noticed that Delano was there, he stood up and made his way over to him.

"I'm guessing that you did not take time to rest." Conner said.

"No, I didn't." Delano said.

"Were you searching for a wife again?"

"Yes."

"How did it go?"

"Not good." Delano said.

Just then, Damien looked at him with tears running down his face.

"Please, tell me that you didn't kill another one." he said.

"She rejected me." Delano said.

"Of course, she rejected you! You're an evil monster!" Damien said.

"I'd be quiet if I were you." Delano said.

"No! You go after married women, and then you wonder why they reject you! Furthermore, there's nothing about you that's pleasant! No one in their right mind would want to be near you! You cause nothing but pain and death! You enjoy other people's suffering, and you never know when to stop!" Damien said.

"Neither do you, otherwise, you'd stop talking." Delano said.

"Who did you kill this time! How many more lives do you have to destroy in order to satisfy your bloodlust!"

"You wouldn't know her." Delano said.

"It doesn't matter! You took her life needlessly. More than likely, some poor man is going to go home to a wife that he'll be missing, but she won't greet him with a hug because she can't because you murdered her!" Damien said.

"The crybaby is going to be in for a real surprise whenever he goes home." Delano said.

"You're sick." Damien said.

"I can't believe that he's around after all this time. I thought for sure that something had happened to him. It turns out, he was alive the entire time, and he had a family. I suppose it no longer matters at this point, since a huge problem has been solved." Delano said.

"What problem?" Damien asked.

"Let's just say that there will be no future warrior. I made sure of that." Delano said.

"I thought you had already eliminated his chance of existing." Zane said.

"That's what I thought, but then I discovered something as I was about to leave. I knew that he was associated with Endymion in some way. He even had purple eyes. Then I found out that he was Aston's grandson. I knew that I couldn't take any chances, and something had to be done about him." Delano said.

"What did you do?" Zane asked.

"Let's just say that someone had a little accident. As I said, his crybaby father will be in for a real surprise whenever he returns to his home." Delano said.

"What?" Damien said.

"He will be someone who will share my misery. He no longer has a family. He'll never have a chance to see his son grow up." Delano said.

"Did you kill a child?" Zane asked.

Delano didn't respond.

"You monster!" Zane said.

He rushed over to Delano and punched him. Then Delano struck him, causing him to fall to the floor.

"Do you think I enjoyed what I did? Think again. Something had to be done. I never knew how that crybaby was related to Endymion, but then, I learned that he's Endymion's grandson, Aston's son. His name is Hugh, and he had a child, named Oliver, who was obviously named after his mother. When I realized who the child was, I knew that he very well could've been the warrior himself. If it wasn't him, there was a high chance of him being born through that child's bloodline. I could not allow that to happen. He had to be eliminated." Delano said.

"You can't stoop any lower than you did. You murdered a child. You shed innocent blood. You disgust me and I think I'm going to be sick." Zane said.

"I told you already that I had no other choice." Delano said.

"How can you live with yourself knowing that you took the life of a child? How do you sleep at night?" Zane said.

"Usually, I don't sleep at night. I don't need much sleep to function. Anyway, I prefer the nighttime." Delano said.

"Of course you do. That's what most evil creatures would prefer. It matches your cold, dark heart." Damien said.

"For your information, I don't just go out during the night. I go out whenever I need to, day or night." Delano said.

With an unhappy expression on his face, Delano left the dungeon, leaving his prisoners behind.

Chapter 16

Oliver's twin brother, Obadiah, was walking up the stairs. When he approached his mother's room, he knocked on the door.

"Mommy, are you in there?" Obadiah asked.

There was no response, so he tried the door, but it wouldn't open. Obadiah sighed before he went to his room to see if his brother was there.

"Oliver?" Obadiah said.

He left the room to search for his family members.

"Mommy? Oliver?" Obadiah said.

He searched each of the rooms upstairs, but there was no sign of either of them. Then he went downstairs to search for them.

"Mommy? Oliver? Where are you?" Obadiah said.

He searched each room downstairs, but he didn't find them. He decided to go outside to search for them. As he walked around the house, he spotted Oliver on the ground, motionless.

"Oliver? Oliver!" Obadiah said.

He rushed over to his brother to see if he was alright. When he approached him, he got down beside him and shook him.

"Oliver? Wake up." Obadiah said.

Oliver wouldn't respond. Obadiah's eyes welled up with tears.

"Oliver? Why won't you wake up?" Obadiah said.

He wiped the tears that streamed down his face before he stood up. Obadiah ran to his grandparents' house and knocked on the door. His grandmother, Rose, answered the door shortly afterward.

"Obadiah, what's wrong?" she asked.

Obadiah sobbed as he looked at his grandmother.

"Grandmother, please, help me. I don't know where mommy is. She's gone, and something's wrong with Oliver. He's outside, and he won't wake up." Obadiah said.

Rose rushed out of the house, and she followed Obadiah to where he had found Oliver. When Rose approached the unconscious child, she picked him up and carried him into her house. Obadiah followed her inside, and they went upstairs. Rose put Oliver on a bed in one of the rooms.

"What's wrong with him?" Obadiah asked.

"I don't know." Rose said.

Obadiah made his way to Oliver's bedside and sat down. He hugged his brother as he wept over him.

"I'm going to try to find help." Rose said.

She then left the room and went outside. The first thing she did was go to Hugh's house to see if Olivia was there. She knocked on the door before she opened it.

"Olivia?" Rose said.

There was no response. She searched every room in the house, but there was no sign of Olivia anywhere. Then she went upstairs to check the bedrooms, but she couldn't find her. When she tried to open the door to Olivia's room, she discovered that it was locked.

"Olivia?" Rose said.

There was no response. Rose rushed down the stairs, and then she went outside. Just then, she spotted the men who were returning. Without hesitation, Rose rushed over to them. Kurtis knew right away that something was wrong.

"Something is wrong with Oliver. Obadiah came to me in tears, telling me that his brother was outside, and he wouldn't wake up. I found him unconscious. He's at my house right now." Rose said.

Kurtis glanced at Hugh, who had an expression of devastation on his face. Aston teleported everyone to his home. They went to the room where Oliver was, and Hugh rushed over to the bed where his son was. Obadiah looked at his father with tears running down his face.

"Daddy." Obadiah said.

He then hugged Hugh, who broke down in tears. Hugh looked at Oliver as tears ran down his face.

"Oliver, my son. What has happened to you? Has someone done something to you?" he said.

He wept as he hugged his son. Kurtis made his way over to Hugh, and then he glanced at him before he tried to heal Oliver. Tears filled Kurtis' eyes as he realized that the child was not responding. He refused to give up even though he felt his energy leaving him. The others who were there had expressions of devastation on their faces as they glanced at one another, and then they looked down at the floor.

A tear trickled down Kurtis' face as he looked at Hugh.

"I'm sorry, son. He won't respond." Kurtis said.

Hugh cupped his hands to his face as he wept bitterly for his son.

"Where's Olivia?" Aston asked.

"I don't know. I looked for her, but I couldn't find her." Rose said.

Kurtis and Aston looked at one another before Aston vanished, taking Kurtis and Steve with him. He teleported to Hugh's house, where they searched for Olivia.

"Olivia?" Kurtis said.

The three men searched the rooms, but they couldn't find her. They went upstairs to look for her. When they tried the door to Olivia's room, they discovered that it was locked, so Aston teleported them into the room. Their hearts sank when they spotted Olivia on the bed. Kurtis rushed over to her to see if she was alright. He closed his eyes as he fought back tears. Then he looked at Aston and Steve with a sorrowful expression on his face.

"She's dead." Kurtis said.

"What happened?" Steve asked.

"It was a bite." Kurtis said.

"Poor Hugh. He's already dealing with what happened to his son. Now, he's going to have to hear that his wife was murdered?" Steve said.

"I'm going to see how Veda's doing." Kurtis said.

"Right. I'll see how Jasmine is doing. I haven't seen her in days. It feels more like years." Steve said.

The three men left Hugh's house. Kurtis went to his home while Steve went to his house. Aston waited outside for both of them. When Kurtis arrived at his home, he went inside right away.

"Honey, I'm home." Kurtis said.

There was no response.

"Veda?" Kurtis said.

He began to worry as he searched his house. Tension rose inside him as he found no sign of her. Then he rushed outside.

"Aston, Veda is missing." Kurtis said.

Just then, Steve approached them with tears running down his face.

"Steve, are you alright?" Kurtis asked.

"No. Jasmine is dead." Steve said.

Then he looked right at Kurtis as he spoke.

"I also found Veda in my house. I'm so sorry, Kurtis. She's also dead. Both of them have bites on them." Steve said.

"No." Kurtis said.

He rushed to Steve's house, with Steve and Aston following him. When Kurtis approached Steve's house, he went right inside.

"Where are they?" Kurtis asked.

"They're upstairs in my room." Steve said.

Kurtis rushed up the stairs, with Aston and Steve following him. When he approached the room, he went inside and spotted his wife on the floor.

"No!" Kurtis said.

He rushed over to her, and then he got down beside her before he broke down in tears.

"Why?" Kurtis said.

He cupped his hands to his face as he wept even harder.

"I'm going to go back to my home. I suppose I'm going to have to break the news to Hugh. I'm not looking forward to it." Aston said.

Then Kurtis stood up.

"I'll come with you." he said.

"So will I." Steve said.

The three of them went back to Aston's house. None of them were ready to tell Hugh about Olivia. When they approached the room where he was, they looked at one another before they went inside.

"Son." Aston said.

Hugh looked at his father with tear-filled eyes.

"There's something that I need to tell you. I think it would be best if we step into another room." Aston said.

"Daddy, don't leave me." Obadiah said.

"Stay here with your grandmother." Hugh said.

He along with Aston, Kurtis, and Steve stepped out of the room and went into another room.

"Son, while we were out, we discovered that there were three people who had been murdered." Aston said.

"Could this get any worse?" Hugh asked.

He then glanced at Kurtis and Steve.

"One of them was Veda and another one was Jasmine." Aston said.

"I'm so sorry." Hugh said.

Then he glanced at his father, who had a sorrowful expression on his face.

"Who was the third victim?" Hugh asked.

He could see that his father was fighting back tears. Then, he looked at Kurtis and Steve and noticed that they were also holding back tears. Hugh's eyes welled up with tears as he looked at his father.

"Father, please, don't tell me what I fear you're about to tell me. I can't deal with it." Hugh said.

"I'm very sorry, son." Aston said.

"No." Hugh said.

At that moment, he broke down and wept. Aston hugged his son, who was beside himself with grief.

Chapter 17

That evening, Olivia, Veda, and Jasmine were laid to rest. It was a sorrowful time for the people of the community, especially for Kurtis, Steve, and Hugh.

Afterward, the three of them went back to Aston's home to see how Oliver was doing. Kurtis shook his head as he looked at the child, and then he looked at Hugh.

"I wish there was something I could do for him. I'm afraid that he's slipping away." Kurtis said.

Hugh cupped his hands to his face as he wept.

"I feel like my entire life is falling apart. What have I done to deserve this?" Hugh said.

"Don't think like that. You've done nothing wrong." Kurtis said.

"Will we ever find the one who's behind this?" Hugh asked.

"I think the real question is, will he ever give himself up?" Kurtis said.

With an unhappy expression on his face, Hugh glanced down at the floor.

"I know that you don't want to hear it because he's your grandfather, but he needs to face the consequences of his actions. He's murdering people. He cannot get away with that. Frankly, I'm disappointed in him. When he was young, most of us thought highly of him. We never thought in our wildest dreams that he would cause this much destruction. He must be stopped." Kurtis stopped.

Hugh cupped his hands to his face as he wept. At that moment, he felt that things had gone from bad to worse.

"I'm sorry, son. I know that it's difficult, but it's the truth. For all we know, he may have been the one who did something to Oliver. He went too far. Something must be done." Kurtis said.

Hugh looked at Oliver as tears ran down his face. He knew that something had to be done, but he didn't want to believe that his grandfather was the one who was behind the deaths or whatever it was that happened to his son.

Chapter 18

It was late in the night when Endymion and Liam returned. Both of them were frustrated because they had no success in finding Delano or the people who had gone missing. Endymion started to fear the worst, even though he didn't want to believe it. As Liam glanced at Endymion, he could tell that he had something on his mind.

"Something isn't right." Endymion said.

"What is it?" Liam asked.

"I feel like something went wrong while we were gone."

"What should we do?" Liam asked.

Suddenly, Endymion had a vision.

"Oh no." he said.

"What is it?" Liam asked.

Endymion and Liam vanished and ended up at the grave site where he spotted the resting spots of Olivia, Veda, and Jasmine.

"No." Endymion said.

"What happened?" Liam asked.

"He was here and he murdered three people. One of them was my brother's wife, and another one was my grandson's wife." Endymion said.

He wept for the three women who had been laid to rest. As his tears fell, flowers came up from the ground.

"I'm so sorry." Liam said.

"Does he know when I leave the area? Had I been here, I could've stopped it." Endymion said.

"Don't blame yourself. You've been trying to stop him. We both have."

"Yes, but it's not enough. He continues to kill people and destroy people's lives."

"It's too bad the people of this community couldn't help us."

"I know, however, we both know how it is. They prefer to blame me for the things that go wrong. I wasn't even here, yet I'm sure they'll find a way to twist it to make it look and sound like I'm the one who caused it." Endymion said.

Then he sighed as he glanced around.

"I want to check on Hugh and his family. I want to see how they're doing." Endymion said.

He and Liam vanished from the grave site and went to Hugh's place, but he found that there was no one there. Then he decided to go to Aston's house. Endymion and Liam glanced at one another before they went upstairs. They went to the room where Hugh, Oliver, and Obadiah were. Endymion winced as he suddenly felt intense pain throughout his body.

"What's wrong?" Liam asked.

"Something's wrong with someone in this room. I can feel it." Endymion said.

As he walked toward the bed, the pain intensified. Endymion glanced at Hugh, who was asleep on a chair. Obadiah was asleep in Hugh's arms.

Endymion's eyes filled with tears as he glanced at Oliver.

"Is it the child that's on the bed?" Liam asked.

"Yes. He's dying. Something terrible has happened to him." Endymion said.

Suddenly, he had a vision of Oliver falling from the window.

"He fell out of a window at his home. He was pushed." Endymion said.

When he approached the bed, he sat down as tears ran down his face.

"He doesn't have much time. He continues to slip away. It's not too late, for I can fix this. I can reverse the damage that has been done. I can mend what has been broken. I will see to it that he lives. Tonight, he will not die." Endymion said.

Then he tried to heal Oliver. At first, the child didn't respond.

"Come on, my son. You are stronger than this. Together we can overcome this." Endymion said.

He continued to try to heal Oliver. For a moment, it seemed hopeless, but then, he responded. Oliver was healed, and it was as though he had never fallen from the window. Endymion made it, so Oliver remained asleep. He picked him up and hugged him as he wept. Then he kissed his forehead. He was happy that the child had pulled through.

"Will he be alright?" Liam asked.

"He has been healed. I caused him to stay asleep because he needs the rest. The entire family is going through a difficult time with the loss of my grandson's wife."

"That's so sad." Liam said.

Endymion carefully placed Oliver back on the bed, and then he gave him another kiss on his forehead.

"Sleep well, my child. I will make sure you have a pleasant dream." Endymion said.

He put his hand on Oliver's forehead as he gave him a good dream. Then he glanced at Hugh, who was awake.

"Grandfather?" Hugh said.

"Your son will be fine. He's asleep now. He has been healed and he will live." Endymion said.

Hugh started to cry tears of joy because he was relieved that his son would not die. He got up, put Obadiah on the bed, and then he picked Oliver up. Hugh hugged his son tightly as he wept. He kissed his son's forehead even as he remained asleep.

"I want you to know how sorry I am about your loss. I wish I would've been here to stop it. I was trying to find the one who was responsible for the things that have been happening. I also searched for the people that had gone missing. I don't want to give up hope. I don't want to believe that they are all dead. I feel terrible for not being here. Unfortunately, he must have shown up while I was away." Endymion said.

A tear trickled down his face as he looked at his grandson.

"I'm sorry, son." Endymion said.

Hugh put Oliver down on the bed, and then he looked at Endymion before he made his way over to him. When he approached him, he looked him in the eyes for a moment before he hugged him as he wept.

"Don't blame yourself for what happened to Olivia. I'm not blaming you for it. I know that it's not your fault. I also know that you're not the one who's kidnapping and murdering people."

"I have been trying to stop the one who's been doing these things. Unfortunately, I'm failing, meanwhile, he's murdering people who I care about. It almost makes me feel powerless. How I want to stop him, but it seems like there's no victory for me."

"I know that you've been trying to put a stop to it. I want to thank you for what you did for Oliver. You saved his life. You have no idea how much joy that brings me.

"Regardless of what everyone here thinks of me, I try to take care of my people. It's all I've ever wanted to do. Unfortunately, they will never accept me. Instead, they continue to blame me for everything that's gone wrong." Endymion said.

He glanced at Oliver, and then he sighed as he looked at Hugh.

"I should probably go back home. I know that I'm not welcome here." Endymion said.

"Grandfather, please, don't leave."

"You and I both know that I'm not welcome here."

"It's not fair. I know you're not the one causing all the trouble. I don't know why they can't see that."

"Unfortunately, they're blind to the truth."

"Well, I'm not. I love you, grandfather. I don't want you to go. Please, stay, at least until the morning."

"Very well. As for you, I think you should try to get some rest. You've had a long, stressful day." Endymion said.

Hugh walked over to the chair where he had fallen asleep earlier and sat down. Endymion caused Hugh to fall asleep, and he gave him a good dream, just as he did to Oliver. Endymion glanced at Obadiah before he gave him a good dream. Then he spotted another chair that was in the room, and he walked over to it and sat down. There was another chair in the room, where Liam sat down. It wasn't long after that when everything became quiet, and it remained that way for the rest of the night.